Finding Tinker Bell

a Never Girls adventure

through the dark forest

written by Kiki Thorpe

Illustrated by Jana Christy

A STEPPING STONE BOOK™

RANDOM HOUSE 🏠 NEW YORK

For Abigail —K.T.
For Sophia, who started as my Gabby
and is now my Mia —J.C.

Library of Congress Cataloging-in-Publication Data is available upon request.

ISBN 978-0-7364-3651-9 (trade)—ISBN 978-0-7364-8183-0 (lib. bdg.)—
ISBN 978-0-7364-3652-6 (ebook)

rhcbooks.com

Printed in the United States of America

10 9 8 7 6 5 4 3 2 1

This book has been officially leveled by using the F&P Text Level Gradient™ Leveling System.

Never Land...
and Beyond

Far away from the world we know, on the distant Never
Sea, lies an island called Never Land. It is a place full of
magic, where mermaids sing, fairies play, and children
never grow up. Adventures happen every day, and
anything is possible.

Though many children have heard of Never Land,
only a special few ever find it. The secret, they know,
lies not in a set of directions but deep within their
hearts, for believing in magic can make extraordinary
things happen. It can open doorways you never even
knew were there.

One day, through an accident of magic, four special
girls found a portal to Never Land right in their own
backyard. The enchanted island became the girls' secret
playground, one they visited every chance they got.
With the fairies of Pixie Hollow as their friends and
guides, they made many magical discoveries.

But Never Land isn't the only island on the Never
Sea. When a special friend goes missing, the girls set
out across the sea to find her. Beyond the shores of
Never Land, they encounter places far stranger than
they ever could have imagined. . . .

This is their story.

Dark Forest

Chapter 1

Of all the strange, magical things that happened to her on Never Land, the one Mia Vasquez could not get used to was flying.

Each time the fairy dust settled over her and she felt its magic—a tickly feeling, like soda bubbles rising inside her—Mia thought, *This time will be different. This time I won't be scared.* And for an instant, as her feet left the ground, it really would seem different. When she floated up, light as a leaf, everything seemed possible.

As soon as she was above the treetops, though, she started to panic. She had to close her eyes and take deep breaths. It was hard not to think about falling.

But what choice did she have? Flying was the only practical way to get around Never Land, especially in the company of fairies. So Mia had learned to hide her fear. Her best friends, Kate McCrady and Lainey Winters, didn't know she was still afraid of flying. Neither did her little sister, Gabby. And she certainly didn't tell the Never fairies. Everyone thought Mia had simply gotten over her fear of heights, the way you get over a cold or a case of the hiccups.

The trick, she found, was never to look

down. Mia kept her eyes on the horizon. She forced a calm expression onto her face. Mia had gotten so good at pretending she wasn't afraid that some days she even managed to convince herself.

Today, unfortunately, was not one of those days.

As Mia flew out over the Never Sea, a knot formed in her stomach. The cold ocean wind tangled her long hair. It raised goose bumps on her arms. Flying over land was hard enough. But flying above water was a thousand times worse. In every direction, all she could see were white-capped waves. Losing her nerve here was not an option.

Keep going, Mia told herself. *Think of Tink!*

Their fairy friend Tinker Bell was lost at sea in a little toy boat. Mia, Kate, Lainey,

Gabby, and four fairies from Pixie Hollow had come out to search for her. But it was an impossible task. Looking for a toy boat in the vast Never Sea was like trying to spot a pinhead in a mountain of sand.

"See anything?" Kate called over the wind.

"Nothing yet," Mia yelled back. Looking for Tink meant looking down, and that was the one thing Mia couldn't do. "Do we even know this is the right way?"

Kate shook her head. "Tink could be anywhere."

It was all Gabby's fault. Mia glared at the back of her sister's head. If Gabby hadn't left their great-grandfather's model boat in Pixie Hollow, Tinker Bell wouldn't have found it. And if Tink hadn't found it and taken it out sailing, they wouldn't be out here looking for her now.

As if she felt Mia's eyes on her, Gabby glanced over her shoulder. She reached out her hand, and Mia's anger softened. She couldn't blame Gabby for wanting to find the boat. Their father had been so upset when Gabby lost it. The *Treasure* was—well, a family treasure. Gabby had promised not to come home without it.

What their father didn't know was that they'd lost it in Never Land. The magical island was the girls' secret.

Mia sped up and caught Gabby's hand. It felt small and warm in her own cold one. She told herself that she was comforting her sister, not the other way around.

Two seagulls, carrying the fairies Fawn, Iridessa, and Silvermist, came circling back toward the girls. The fourth fairy, Rosetta, was riding on Gabby's shoulder.

"Let's turn around!" Iridessa shouted. The wind almost carried her voice away.

But Mia heard her. Relief spread through Mia's chest.

"We can't stop looking!" Gabby piped

up. "Tink's still out here somewhere!"

"I don't think she could have come this far. Not in such a small boat," Silvermist said.

"We won't stop looking," Fawn reassured Gabby. "But we don't know which way Tink went. We need to warm up and rest. Then we'll try another direction."

The group turned back toward Never Land, but the wind was against them now. Mia felt as if someone were holding her shoulders, trying to push her backward. Ahead, she could see Never Land's shore with its thin white thumbnail of sand. Only a few more minutes and her feet would be on the ground.

Abruptly, the air grew colder. Mia looked up and saw that a dark cloud had moved across the sun.

They had seen the same cloud earlier. Mia was sure of it. From the ground, it had seemed little and harmless, a distant smudge in the bright blue sky. But up here, in the air, it looked bigger and darker.

A raindrop splashed against Mia's face.

The search party stopped and treaded air. They were at the edge of the storm. Ahead, rain hung like a curtain between them and Never Land.

"We'd better not fly through it!" Fawn shouted from the back of her seagull.

"Let's take the long way around," Iridessa agreed. "We can fly north over the tip of the island and come in from the west."

Mia's heart sank. That would mean at least another hour of flying, maybe more.

And they were so close! "It's only a little rain," she argued.

"I don't like the look of that cloud," Rosetta said from Gabby's shoulder.

Mia saw her friends hesitate. If she didn't do something quickly, they'd agree to take the long route. "You guys fly around if you want," she said with a boldness she didn't feel. "I'm going ahead." Without waiting for an answer, she plunged into the storm.

Behind her, Mia heard someone shouting her name, but she couldn't tell who it was. The cold raindrops stung her skin and blurred her eyes. She could no longer see Never Land's shore. Was she even going in the right direction?

Mia paused to get her bearings. Then she made her worst mistake: she looked down.

At the sight of the choppy sea below, Mia's confidence fled. She dropped like a stone.

She screamed, but the sound was lost in the wind. The sea sped toward her. Mia braced herself for the cold water.

Then came a blinding flash. The cloud above her blazed from within. The air frizzled with electricity.

And suddenly everything flipped. That was the only word Mia could use to describe it. The world seemed to turn itself upside down.

A second later, she came down hard on dry sand.

Chapter 2

As a garden-talent fairy, Rosetta consid-
ered herself to be something of an expert
on clouds. She knew which thunderheads
held precious rain and which were all
bluster. She could tell wispy clouds that
signaled a sudden cold snap apart from
the ones that marked a fair-weather day.

But she'd never seen a cloud like this
one. It was greenish black, so dark it
seemed to suck light right out of the sky.

A cloud with a secret. That's what Rosetta was thinking when, with a deafening crack of thunder, Mia vanished.

Gabby screamed, "Mia!"

Rosetta had never had a sister, so she could only imagine it was sisterly love that made Gabby do what she did next. Instead of flying away from the menacing cloud—which, in Rosetta's opinion, was the only sensible thing to do—she flew toward it. All Rosetta could do was hold on tight as they dove into the heart of the storm.

The rain slashed down. The wind seemed to tear at them with claws. Rosetta clung to Gabby's collar, terrified. She imagined herself blowing away like a milkweed seed.

"Slow down!" she cried.

Gabby either didn't hear her or didn't care to listen for she sped up.

Then came a flash and a boom so shattering that it seemed to knock the whole world out of alignment. The sea, the land, and the sky looked like pieces of a jigsaw puzzle that had been knocked askew.

The impression lasted only an instant. In the blink of an eye, the world put itself back together.

But something was wrong. The earth was now where the sky should be. And they were falling toward it.

"Fly, Gabby! Fly!" Rosetta tugged helplessly on the girl's collar. The costume fairy wings Gabby always wore buzzed like the wings of a dying bee as they plummeted down—or was it up?—through the cloud.

Rosetta squeezed her eyes shut.

Thump. Gabby came down so hard that Rosetta bounced off her shoulder. She landed headfirst in warm sand.

Rosetta got up, spitting sand. Two feet away, Gabby lay still on the ground. Her eyes were closed.

Rosetta gasped and fluttered to her. She pinched the girl's cheek.

Gabby opened her eyes and blinked. "Where's Mia?" she asked, sitting up.

"I don't know." Rosetta looked around. They were on a beach ringed by jagged black rocks. To one side lay a flat green sea. To the other, a dark forest. A rust-colored sun hovered just above the

horizon. Strangely, the ugly storm cloud had vanished.

"I don't like the look of that forest," Rosetta said.

"Gabby! Rosetta!" Mia came running across the sand. She gave Gabby a big hug. "What happened?" she asked Rosetta.

"I don't know," Rosetta said again.

They heard a shout. Kate and Lainey were making their way up the beach. Iridessa flew alongside them.

"Well, that was lucky, huh?" said Kate when she reached them.

"*What* was lucky?" Rosetta asked. So far, nothing about this trip seemed lucky.

"I thought we were goners when that lightning started. I guess Never Land was closer than we thought." Kate pushed her bangs away from her green eyes. "Where are Fawn and Silvermist?"

They looked up and down the beach. There was no sign of the two fairies or their seagull.

"Weren't they flying next to you?" Lainey asked Iridessa.

"Yes," the light-talent fairy replied. "But my seagull threw me when it saw the lightning. I didn't see where they went."

"I think the bigger question is, where are *we*?" Rosetta said.

Kate looked surprised. "Aren't we in Never Land?"

"Not any part I've ever seen," Rosetta said.

Hands on her hips, Iridessa surveyed their surroundings. "I'm going to look around." She fluttered off with a wave.

Mia turned to Gabby. "Do you still have that map?"

Gabby dug in her pocket for the tiny scroll. They'd found the map in Tinker Bell's workshop just after she disappeared. It was a simple map of Never Land and the surrounding sea. But, strangely, it had been labeled *Shadow Island*. So far, it was the only clue they had to where Tinker Bell might have gone.

Gabby unrolled the map and gasped. "Oh! Look!"

The map had changed. Never Land was gone, as if it had been erased. In its place, an unfamiliar island was sketched in.

"It's a magic map!" Gabby exclaimed.

"But what does it mean?" Lainey asked.

"Maybe we found Shadow Island!" Kate said.

"But Silvermist told us Shadow Island is just a myth," Lainey said. "And anyway, we didn't see any other islands when we were out searching."

"The storm!" Mia exclaimed. "We flew into the storm, and we ended up here. That must be what happened."

"Like a portal!" Kate said.

Mia nodded. "And Silvermist and Fawn flew around it. That's why they aren't here. I wish I'd never—"

"Hey! Over here!" A shout cut Mia off. Iridessa was calling to them from up the beach.

They hurried over to her. Where the beach gave way to forest, the ground was soggy. Iridessa pointed to a line of tiny marks in the mud.

"They look like footprints!" said Kate.

"*Fairy* footprints," added Iridessa.

The friends looked at each other. Lainey raised her eyebrows. "Do you think it could be—"

"Tinker Bell!" the others exclaimed.

"Maybe the storm pushed

her here, too," Mia said hopefully.

The tracks disappeared into the forest. The friends peered into the tangled undergrowth. The sense of unease Rosetta had felt since they landed grew stronger.

"I think we have to go in there," Iridessa said.

Rosetta sighed. "I was afraid you were going to say that."

Chapter 3

Iridessa led the way since she had the strongest glow. The woods lay deep in shadow. Only a few weak shafts of sunlight peeked through the dense canopy. Weaving between the tree trunks, Iridessa was the brightest thing in the forest.

They moved through the undergrowth, calling Tink's name. Their voices seemed small and weak among the towering trees. The woods were eerily silent.

Silent, but not empty, Rosetta thought. She couldn't shake the feeling that they were being watched.

To distract herself, she studied the plants. Hardly any flowers grew in the shadowy forest. But what a lot of mushrooms! Rosetta had never seen so many different kinds. There were bright orange mushrooms that looked like coral. Mushrooms shaped like teacups, complete with tea-colored water inside. She saw mushrooms as small as pinheads and others as big as ostrich eggs. There were tall mushrooms with fringes and fat ones that looked like they were trimmed in lace. Here was one that oozed red jelly. And there—

Rosetta did a double take. "Stop!"

The girls walking behind her bumped into one another. Iridessa came fluttering back. "What's wrong? What happened?" she asked.

Rosetta pointed at a fungus with a pale blue cap and a stubby stem. "We passed that before."

"Pretty!" Gabby reached out a finger to touch it.

Mia pulled her hand back. "Don't! It might be poisonous."

"Are you sure it's the same one?" Kate asked Rosetta. "Lots of mushrooms look alike."

"Not to me, they don't," Rosetta replied. "See how the edge of the cap is bent? I'm sure it's the same one."

Iridessa folded her arms. "Are you saying I'm going in circles?" she huffed. "Because you should try leading if you think it's so—"

"I didn't say we're going in circles," Rosetta broke in. "I think that toadstool is following us."

Silence. Everyone peered at the mushroom. Was it Rosetta's imagination, or was it standing a little taller?

"I think it's holding its breath," Gabby whispered.

Mia rolled her eyes. "Be serious, Gabby. It just looks like a regular mushroom."

"We can't let our imagination run away with us," Lainey agreed.

"That's right," Kate said. "The sooner we find Tink, the sooner we can get back to

Never Land. Iridessa, which way now?"

She turned, but the light-talent fairy was gone.

"Iridessa?" Kate looked around. "Where did she go?"

"She was here a second ago," said Mia.

They peered into the trees. Without Iridessa's bright glow, the forest seemed darker than ever.

"Iridessa, if this is a joke, we don't think it's funny," Rosetta called.

There was no answer.

"Maybe she's scouting up ahead," Kate said.

"But which way?" Mia asked. There was no clear path through the forest. They were surrounded by ferns and vines.

"Let's each pick a direction," Kate

suggested. "Shout as soon as you spot her. She can't have gone very far."

They fanned out like spokes on a wheel. Rosetta flew between the leaves of a giant fern and over a rotting log. The trees here were twice as big as the Home Tree, the giant maple that housed all the fairies in Pixie Hollow. Thick moss grew around their trunks, giving the forest an ancient feel.

There's something strange about this place, Rosetta thought. It wasn't just that the plants were unusual. She felt an immense presence. It was watching, waiting. What was it?

"Iridessa?" she called.

Rosetta glanced over her shoulder. She could hear the girls crashing through

the leaves. *They sound like elephants,* Rosetta thought. But it was comforting to know they were close.

She flew a little farther. "Iridessa?"

Rosetta landed on a broad leaf. She was afraid of going too far and getting lost. She had just decided to turn back when, suddenly, the leaf she was standing on folded around her. Rosetta was too surprised to cry out. Darkness engulfed her from all sides.

Chapter 4

Mia was watching Rosetta out of the corner of her eye when the fairy's glow suddenly vanished.

Had she flown out of view? Or had her glow winked out for a second? That sometimes happened when a fairy was surprised.

"Rosetta?" Mia called. "Are you all right?"

There was no answer.

Mia shivered. She didn't want to be

alone in this strange place. She turned and hurried back to the spot where she'd left her friends, yelling, "Guys, where are you?"

Mia heard leaves rustling. One by one, Kate, Lainey, and Gabby emerged from the forest. "Did you find Iridessa?" Kate asked.

"No, and now Rosetta's gone, too," Mia said.

"Gone? Are you sure?" Lainey asked.

Mia nodded. "I could see her light and then it just . . . went out. She didn't answer when I called her."

The girls looked at her in alarm. Mia knew what they were thinking. The fairies would never just leave them. Something terrible must have happened.

Gabby reached for her. "Mia, I'm scared."

"Me too." Mia grasped Gabby's hand and pulled her closer. The four girls huddled together.

"What should we do now?" Lainey whispered.

They all turned to look at Kate. She always had a plan.

Kate licked her lips. Her green eyes flicked around the woods. "We . . . we have to look for them," she said. "Everybody, stay close. Whatever we find, we'll face it together. Okay?"

The girls nodded solemnly. Holding tight to each other, they moved deeper into the trees.

If the forest had been gloomy before,

now it seemed downright sinister. Without the fairies' light, the shadows seemed to press closer. Mia felt eyes watching them.

I wish I'd never flown into that storm!

Mia replayed the moment over and over in her mind. If she'd only listened when the fairies said to fly around the rain, they would be safe in Pixie Hollow now. Just thinking of it made a lump form in her throat.

Mia was so caught up in her thoughts that she didn't notice the tiny creature perched in front of her until she almost walked into it.

She let out a squeal and jumped backward into Kate. Startled, Kate bumped into Lainey. Then all the girls were yelling and bumping into each other.

Lainey gasped. "What's the matter?"

Mia pointed to the leaf. "A big freaky bug!"

Kate peered at it. "That's no bug!"

Looking closer, Mia saw that Kate was right—it wasn't a bug. It was a tiny man. He wore a hat made from a mushroom cap and a coat of leaves. In his arms he held a long asparagus stalk, which he pointed at Kate.

"Look!" Lainey cried. Another tiny man had appeared on a tree root. This one wore a red toadstool cap with white spots. When Lainey crouched down to look at him, he shook his asparagus at her menacingly.

With a faint rustle, dozens of sprites emerged from the forest. They were about

the size of fairies, but they had no wings. They had worm-pale skin and sharp black eyes, and they all wore hats made of mushrooms. Some were wide-brimmed, like sunhats. Others were brown or red with white spots and fit snugly, like caps. The sprites surrounded the girls, aiming asparagus spears at their ankles.

Mia spotted a familiar pale blue cap.

"Rosetta was right. That mushroom *was* following us!" she murmured.

"What do they want?" Lainey asked.

"Maybe they know where the fairies are!" Kate turned to the first sprite they'd seen, the one standing on the fern leaf. "I'm Kate," she said slowly, pointing her thumb at her chest. "We mean you no harm. We just want to find our fairy friends."

The sprite stared at her, unblinking.

Kate made a fluttering motion with her hands. "Fairies?" she repeated. When the sprite didn't reply, she frowned and leaned closer. "Do. You. Understand?"

The sprite lifted his asparagus and poked her in the nose.

Kate's head snapped back. "Hey!"

Mia giggled. "I guess they don't speak

your language, Kate. They're kind of cute, though."

No sooner had the words left her mouth than she felt a jab on her ankle. "What?" Mia looked down. A band of sprites surrounded her foot. They poked her with their spears.

"Quit it!" Gabby exclaimed. The sprites were attacking Gabby's feet, too. "Mia, make them stop!"

Mia stomped her foot, and the sprites scattered a few inches. "Go on. Leave us alone!" She raised her foot again in a threatening way.

"Mia, don't!" Lainey said. "I think they're trying to tell us something. Look."

A band of sprites were leading the way into the forest. They looked back over their shoulders at the girls.

"They want us to follow them," Lainey explained.

"Why should we?" Mia said. "They're not exactly friendly."

"I think we should," Kate said. "We're not getting anywhere on our own. Maybe we'll learn something about this weird place."

Mia felt another poke on her ankle. She swatted away the asparagus and scowled. "All right, all right. We're coming," she snapped.

The sprites led the way, and the girls followed, tripping over tree roots and crashing through leaves. The deeper they went, the darker the forest became. Scraps of fog floated among the trees like silent ghosts.

Mia shivered and rubbed her arms. She noticed that the sprites moved furtively. Every now and then they glanced up toward the treetops. But when she followed their gaze, all she could see were branches. What were the sprites watching for?

They had been walking for only a short time when, without a word, the sprites came to a halt.

"Why are we stopping?" Kate asked.

They were standing in a glade formed by enormous trees. Mushrooms and toadstools dotted the ground between the thick, mossy tree roots.

Mia blinked and looked again. That large mushroom had windows and a door!

Now she noticed that what she'd mistaken for a vine was actually a bridge connecting two tree stumps. A tiny face peeked from a window in one of the stumps, then quickly vanished again.

"I think this is where they live!" she said.

Mia studied the forest with careful eyes. As she did, a tiny village seemed to emerge—slowly, then all at once. The biggest mushrooms were little houses. Tiny white fungi formed graceful paths like stepping-stones. A fungus stairway encircled a tree trunk, leading up to a tiny lookout hut.

A furry gray moth flitted past. A beetle crawled over the toe of Mia's shoe and continued on its way, carrying a bundle of pine needles on its back.

The sprites' home reminded Mia a little of Pixie Hollow. Instead of flowers and butterflies, they had mushrooms and moths. But something else was different, too.

There's no light! Mia realized. Not so much as a firefly lantern glowed in any of the windows.

An older sprite walked slowly toward them. She had a pale, wrinkled face and wore a cloak made of rough brown leaves. Her mushroom cap had five pointed tips.

"Is she the queen?" Gabby whispered.

"Maybe," Mia whispered back. The sprite's cap did look sort of crownlike.

The sprite stopped when she was about a foot in front of them. "Welcome," she said.

"You can talk?" Kate cried.

The sprite looked amused. "We speak, yes," she said. "But we don't always choose to."

"Where are we?" Lainey asked.

"The village of Low Ones," the sprite replied. "I am Ersa. We welcome you, friends of the Brilliant Ones."

"Brilliant Ones?" asked Mia.

"The bringers of light," Ersa said.

The girls exchanged confused looks. "We don't know any, er, bringers of light," Kate said. "We're just looking for our friends."

Ersa turned and began to walk away. "Come," she said over her shoulder.

The girls followed her to a hollow log covered with moss. A warm light shone through the cracks in the wood. It was the brightest light they'd seen since they'd entered the forest. A few sprites armed with asparagus spears stood outside.

Ersa motioned the guards aside. At the opening to the hollow log, she stopped and beckoned the girls closer.

Cautiously, Mia knelt to look inside. She gasped in surprise.

Chapter 5

"Rosetta!" Mia exclaimed. "Iridessa!" The two fairies were the source of the warm yellow glow.

"You found us!" exclaimed Rosetta. Her glow brightened with joy.

"We were worried we'd never see you again!" said Iridessa.

"Us too," said Kate, leaning down. "But what are you doing here?"

The fairies told the same story. They'd

been flying through the forest, and when they paused on a leaf, they'd been captured and brought to the sprites' village.

Mia whirled toward the old sprite. "*You* kidnapped our friends?"

"For their own good," Ersa said.

"Good?" Kate snapped. "You scared everyone half to death." She turned to the fairies. "Come on. We're getting you out of here."

"We're right behind you," Iridessa said. The fairies fluttered out of the log.

"No!" Ersa cried. "Stop!"

A roaring sound came from above, as if the treetops were caught in a sudden windstorm. The noise was enough to stop the girls in their tracks.

"What?" Mia looked back to Ersa for

an explanation. But all the sprites had disappeared.

Suddenly, something hard came hurtling down and hit the top of Lainey's head.

"Ow!" she cried.

Another hard object followed. In seconds, everyone was being pelted with falling debris.

"Take cover!" Iridessa shouted.

The fairies dove for shelter in the undergrowth. The girls, who were too big to hide under anything, crouched and covered their heads with their arms. The objects stung where they struck. As they collected on the ground, Mia realized that they weren't rocks, as she'd first thought. They were small green pinecones.

In a few moments, the barrage let up. The girls shakily rose to their feet.

"What was *that*?" Kate asked.

"The Great Ones," Ersa said, emerging from under a large mushroom.

"Great Ones?" Rosetta asked.

Ersa glanced warily at a nearby sapling. Mia didn't see anything unusual about the tree, but the sprite said, "There are spies everywhere. Let's find a safer place to talk. But you must hide your glows." She started away through the forest, scurrying like a mouse.

Without knowing what else to do, the girls and fairies followed. The fairies dimmed their glows to a dull light.

As they passed through the village, more sprites emerged from their hiding places to stare, gaping at the group of friends with wide eyes and open mouths.

It's not us they're looking at, Mia realized. *It's the fairies.* The sprites were transfixed by the fairies' light. One bold sprite even reached out to touch Rosetta's rose-petal dress as she passed.

"They've never seen Brilliant Ones before," Ersa said.

"Why does she keep calling the fairies 'Brilliant Ones'?" Lainey whispered to Mia.

Mia shrugged. Everything about this village was odd.

Ersa led them to what looked like a small cave standing alone in the woods. As they got closer, Mia saw that it was the remains of what had once been a massive tree. A fire had gutted it—all that was left

was an enormous hollow stump. It was so big that all four girls could fit inside comfortably. The blackened walls were smooth and polished. Mia guessed the fire had occurred long ago.

Ersa and the fairies sat at a mushroom table inside the hollow, while the girls sat cross-legged behind them. Sprites served them cold mushroom soup in acorn bowls.

Mia clutched the tiny cup with chilled fingers. She wished it were hot. Wasn't there anything warm in this dark, gloomy place?

"The Great Ones are the forest giants," Ersa explained as they ate. "They are the ones who attacked."

"Why?" Kate asked. "Did we do something wrong?"

"They saw your glows," Ersa told the fairies. "The Great Ones will not allow us to have any light. They attack even the tiniest spark."

Iridessa looked aghast. "Why would anyone hate light?"

"We do not know," Ersa said. "It has been that way for as long as we Low Ones can remember."

"That's terrible." Mia tried to imagine living without light. She shivered.

"Why don't you leave?" Lainey asked Ersa.

The sprite's forehead wrinkled. "Leave?"

"Yeah, you could go live at the beach or someplace sunny," Kate suggested.

"Out in the open? Outside the forest?" Ersa looked horrified. "But this is our home!" She turned to the fairies. "Where you come from there is plenty of light, yes?"

"Oh, yes!" said Iridessa. "So much sunlight. And moonlight at night."

"And flowers blooming everywhere," Rosetta chimed in. "Almost every day is spring or summer."

"Tell me more," said Ersa.

So the fairies told her about the Home Tree with its great knothole door and the dozens of fairy rooms lining its branches. They told her about fairy feasts of sun-dried berries and fresh-baked bread. They told her how beautiful Pixie Hollow looked at night, lit up by firefly lanterns.

Ersa closed her eyes, basking in the description as if the words themselves

were warm. "Yes," she said. "Yes, that's
how our village will be. Now that you are
here."

"Us?" Iridessa and Rosetta exclaimed in
unison.

Ersa smiled. "With your light, our
home can be like yours."

"It doesn't work that way," Iridessa tried

to explain. "You need sunlight. And fairy dust. We can't glow or do magic without fairy dust."

"Besides," Rosetta added, "we can't stay."

Ersa's face fell. "Why not?"

"We're looking for our friend, Tinker Bell," Rosetta told her. The fairies explained how Tinker Bell had set out to sea in a toy boat. She'd sailed off early one morning and hadn't been seen since.

"We think she might have gotten caught in the same storm we did," Mia said. "The one that brought us here."

"So, this Tinker Bell is important to you?" Ersa asked.

The girls and fairies nodded. "She's our very good friend," said Rosetta.

Ersa was quiet for a moment. "If you

will not stay, you must do something before you leave."

"What's that?" asked Iridessa.

"The Great Ones live Above." Ersa waved a hand to indicate the forest over their heads. "We Low Ones are small and helpless. We have no way to reach them. But you can fly. You must go to them and ask them to give us light."

Mia almost laughed out loud. This little sprite had a lot of nerve! "You want us to talk to some nasty, light-hating giants? I think we'll pass," she said.

"You must do this," Ersa said firmly.

"We don't have to do anything," Kate said. "You tried to kidnap our friends. I don't see why we should help you at all."

Ersa lifted her chin. "Then we have no

more to discuss." She stood to leave.

As she stepped away, her foot poked out from beneath her long skirt. Her shoe was leaf green with a pom-pom made from dandelion fluff.

The girls and fairies stared. She was wearing Tinker Bell's slipper.

Chapter 6

"Stop!" Mia blocked the sprite's way with her foot. "Where did you get that slipper?" she demanded.

"Our scouts found it on the beach. They brought it to me," Ersa replied.

"Liar!" Kate rose to her full height. "That shoe belongs to our friend Tink. What have you done with her?"

A look of fear flashed across Ersa's face. Mia imagined how Kate must look to her—like a glaring red-faced, freckled giant.

Still the sprite wouldn't give in. "I told you I know nothing of this Tinker Bell," Ersa said. "But if you do as I ask, then the Low Ones will help you."

The girls and fairies looked at one another. Could they trust her?

"She's bluffing," Mia said. "I bet she can't help us."

"Or won't," Iridessa added.

"But she has Tink's shoe!" Gabby argued.

There was a long pause. "Fine. I'll go see the Great Ones," Kate said at last. "I'm not afraid."

Iridessa looked around. "So we'll go. Is everyone in agreement?"

"No, not everyone," Kate said. She

glanced at Ersa and added, "I think we should split up. That way, if—if there's a problem, the rest of us can keep looking for Tink."

Kate is so brave, Mia thought. She wished she could be like her friend, but her heart was jumping in her chest like a scared rabbit.

"Who's with me?" Kate asked.

Mia knew she should say "I am." But the words seemed to stick in her throat. Before she could force them out, Lainey spoke up.

"I'll go."

Everyone looked at her in surprise. Lainey pushed her thick glasses up her nose and looked back at her friends defiantly.

Mia felt a flush of shame. Lainey was younger than she was. *And,* Mia thought, *about ten times braver.*

"I'll go, too," Rosetta said. "If the Great Ones hate light, then Iridessa won't be safe with her light talent."

"Are you sure?" Kate said. "Maybe both of you should stay here just to be safe."

"Why would they bother with a little old garden-talent fairy like me?" Rosetta said, smiling. "Besides, there's something odd about this forest. I don't know what it is, but I want to find out."

Ersa nodded. "Wear this," she said to Rosetta, taking off her own leaf-cloak. "For your protection."

Rosetta slipped on the cloak. With the hood on, her glow was barely visible.

They came out of the cave. "How far up do you think the Great Ones live?" Lainey asked, peering up at the treetops.

"Who knows?" said Kate. "But it might be far. We'll need more fairy dust."

Kate untied the cloth sack that was hanging from her belt loop. The dust-talent fairies had given them extra fairy dust to take on their search for Tink.

At the time, it had seemed like more than enough. But now, looking at the shimmering dust, Mia thought it didn't seem like much at all. Who knew how long it would have to last them?

Kate gave each girl a pinch of the fairy dust. Then she knelt to dole out pinches to the fairies, too.

As she stood to retie the sack to her belt, she tripped over a tree root. She fell against a tree trunk, hitting her head hard.

The girls and fairies rushed to her. "Kate, are you okay?" Mia asked.

"Yeah." Kate tried to rise. But she wobbled and sat down abruptly.

"That does it," Rosetta said. "You can't fly in that condition."

Kate leaned against the trunk. Her face looked pale. "But we have to go see the Great Ones," she said faintly.

Lainey turned to Mia and Gabby with a worried look. "Someone else will come with me, right?"

"I will!" Gabby said.

"No. You stay here and take care of Kate. I'll go." The last thing Mia wanted to do was go find the Great Ones. But after Kate, she was the oldest. She couldn't send her little sister and Lainey off alone.

"You're sure you'll be okay, Mia?" Kate asked as they prepared to leave.

Mia could only nod. She wasn't sure at all. Without Kate, how would she know what to do?

"Be Never fairies at their best," Iridessa told them. It was something fairies said to one another when parting for an important journey. Even though she wasn't really a fairy, the words had a reassuring ring for Mia.

Be like a fairy at her best, Mia told herself.

They rose into the air.

At first the branches were sparse. But as they flew higher, the canopy became dense. Mia passed a long line of ants carrying bits of leaves on one branch. On another, she saw clusters of tiny white flowers growing. The branch had its own little garden!

"More mushrooms," Rosetta remarked, examining a large one growing nearby. "This forest is full of them."

"Look at this!" Lainey called. She was hovering next to an enormous nest.

The others flew over for a closer look. The nest was made of sticks and twigs, and was as big around as a bathtub. Mia tried to imagine the bird that would need a nest that big.

"What could have made it?" Rosetta asked.

"I'm not sure," Lainey said, examining the nest with interest. She liked anything to do with animals. "But see how old and dry the sticks are? Whatever made it hasn't been here for a while."

"Well, that's a relief," Mia said.

They continued upward. "I was wondering," Lainey said as they flew, "what do the Great Ones have against light? I mean, why would they care if the Low Ones have it? From the way Ersa made it sound, they've never even met them."

"Maybe they're just really mean," Mia said. But she thought Lainey was right. It didn't make sense. If the Great Ones were really so great, why would it matter to them if the tiny sprites had a lantern or two?

As the girls flew higher, the air became warmer. Soft sunlight filtered through the pine needles.

Mia was just thinking how much more pleasant it was up here, when she spotted a pair of red eyes staring at her from between two branches.

"Ahh!" She sprang back. A football-sized animal scuttled away along the branch.

"You scared it off." Lainey peered at the hole where the critter had disappeared.

She sounded a little disappointed.

"I know." Mia's face burned. What was wrong with her? She was supposed to be leading, not freaking out at every little thing they came across.

Farther up, they spotted several smaller nests, including one full of gray-feathered chicks. Shiny green beetles crawled over the bark of the tree trunks. At one point, they heard leaves crashing and saw a dark shape swinging away through the branches. But they didn't see anything that could have been called a giant.

At last, they reached the topmost branches. Mia crested the treetops and gasped. "Oh, look!"

The forest rolled before them like a great green sea. Far in the distance they could see dark mountains silhouetted against the sky. In the other direction was the actual sea. It was a slightly deeper shade of green than the forest.

"It reminds me of Never Land," Rosetta said. "But only a little."

Lainey shielded her eyes and looked toward the horizon. "Is it morning or evening?" she asked. "It seems like the sun is in the same place as when we got here."

"But it was on the other side of the ocean before, wasn't it?" Rosetta said. "Or maybe I'm wrong. I'm all turned around."

Mia didn't reply. They had made it all the way to the top of the forest and still hadn't come across the Great Ones. She wasn't sure whether to feel disappointed or relieved.

As if reading her mind, Lainey said, "I guess we should wait and see if any Great Ones come along."

There was nowhere to rest, so they flew back down into the canopy. In the largest tree, Mia found a sturdy branch to sit on.

She had just leaned her back against the tree trunk, when she heard a deep voice. It was so close it seemed to be speaking right into her ear.

"Make yourself at home, why don't you?"

Mia gave a start. She twisted around, looking for the speaker. No one was there.

But as she stared at the tree trunk, the bark suddenly formed into a mouth, nose, and two deep-set eyes.

"Well," said the tree in the same rumbling voice, "what are *you* looking at?"

Chapter 7

Mia screamed and leaped back from the tree trunk. She lost her grip on the narrow branch and tumbled head over heels out of the tree.

She clutched at pine needles to stop her fall, but they slipped through her fingers. Some part of her brain was crying, "Fly! Fly!" But she was too scared to remember how.

Mia might have fallen all the way to

the ground if a branch hadn't caught her squarely across the middle.

"Oof!" Mia grunted. She clung to the branch and squeezed her eyes tight. She was afraid to move an inch.

"Mia." Lainey touched her arm. Mia hadn't even heard her fly down. "Are you all right? Can you fly?"

Mia shook her head.

She heard a soft flutter of wings. Then Rosetta spoke into her other ear. "Try."

Mia squeezed her eyes tighter. She never wanted to fly again. All she wanted was to be safe on the ground.

"You have to try," Rosetta insisted. "Mia, we've found the Great Ones!"

Mia opened her eyes. "We have?"

"The trees," Rosetta said. "It must be

them. They're the biggest things in the forest. Giants."

Cautiously, Mia relaxed her grip. Their mission suddenly seemed a little less frightening. What harm could come of talking to trees?

Be a fairy at her best, Mia reminded herself. She owed it to their friends on the ground. And to Tinker Bell, wherever she was.

"Okay," she said. "I'm ready."

Lainey stretched out her hand, and Mia took it. Together with Rosetta, they flew back up to the branch she'd been sitting on. Mia was surprised to see it wasn't more than a few feet overhead. It had felt as if she'd fallen much farther.

"Rosetta," she whispered, "you'd better let Lainey and me do the talking. If Ersa is right, they might not like fairies."

Rosetta nodded and tightened her hood.

The face in the trunk was still there. Even though its eyes were only hollows, they seemed to bore into Mia. She glanced around and saw that other trees had opened their eyes and were watching them.

Mia swallowed hard and turned back to the first tree. "Are you the Great Ones?"

"Who wants to know?" the tree replied gruffly.

They heard a sigh that sounded like wind whooshing through branches. "Must you speak to them, Magnus?" a nearby tree asked.

"Don't encourage them," said another. "They're only a couple of groundlings."

"What am I supposed to do?" the first tree retorted. "They're in my branches!"

Mia took that as permission to go on. "My name is Mia. This is Lainey and Rosetta. We were sent by the Low Ones."

Mia waited, but the tree said nothing. Was he even listening?

"You know the Low Ones, right? They live in the forest? On the ground?" she asked.

"I know the clouds and rain," the tree called Magnus rumbled. "I know the birds that fly past. I know nothing of these Low Ones."

Mia glanced at Lainey. Was it true? Did the Great Ones really know nothing about the sprites? If so, why had they attacked them?

"It's very dark in the forest," Mia said.

"The Low Ones sent us to ask for more light."

"Just a few lanterns or something," Lainey added.

The trees' frowns deepened.

"Here's the thing," Mia hurried on. "You're blocking all the sunlight. So could you maybe move out of the way?"

Silence. The girls and Rosetta waited.

A tremor started somewhere below. It traveled slowly upward through the trees, growing stronger and stronger, until the branch they were standing on started to shake. Was it an earthquake?

Mia looked around at the other trees. Their mouths were wide open as they shook. Finally, she understood—the trees were laughing at them!

"Move?" Magnus howled. "MOVE? I've

stood here for seven hundred years. I'll stand here for seven hundred more. My roots reach a half mile below the ground. We are the Great Ones. We do not move."

The trees went on laughing. "Let's go," Mia whispered to her friends. "I don't think they're going to help us."

"Wait," Rosetta said. "Before we leave, we have to ask them about Tink. Maybe they've seen her."

Mia waited until the branch she was on stopped swaying. "Great One," she said. "One more thing. We're looking for our friend Tinker Bell. She's a fairy. Have you seen her?"

Magnus let out a long sigh. "I see many things. Who can say?"

"Please!" Rosetta burst out, unable to

stay silent any longer. "Try to think! She has blond hair and a green dress and a lemon-yellow glow—"

As Rosetta flew forward, the hood on her cloak fell back. Her glow shone out, her bright red hair flashing. The tree's eyes widened.

"Spark!" he roared. "Spark!"

"Spark!" the trees around them echoed in alarm.

At once, the treetops began to bend and sway as if they were caught in a terrible windstorm. Their branches rattled violently.

"Spark!" they shrieked.

A bough hit Mia's back. Another caught Lainey across the knees. A twig whistled past Rosetta's wings.

"Let's get out of here!" Mia cried.

They dove down through the trees, dodging the whipping branches. They didn't stop until they reached the lower branches, where the forest was calm.

"What was that about?" Lainey gasped.

Rosetta struggled to catch her breath. "I think they thought I was on fire!"

"Or they thought you *were* fire," Mia

said, putting it together. "They attacked the Low Ones when they saw your glows. Maybe it's not light that they hate—it's *fire.*"

Now it made sense. A single spark could burn a whole forest down. The giant trees were protecting themselves.

Mia thought of the burned-out stump in the sprites' village and shivered. That stump had once been a Great One, too.

"But how do they know?" Lainey asked. "They don't even know who the Low Ones are. How can they see a tiny lantern or a fairy glow from all the way up there?"

"Some trees communicate through their roots," Rosetta said. "They must have some way of alerting one another."

Mia remembered Ersa's comment about

spies and the fearful look she'd given the sapling.

"It's the little trees!" Mia said. "They can see what happens in the forest. They must tell the big ones!"

Lainey looked uneasily up at the giant trees. "Do you think we should try to explain that fairies can't hurt them?"

Mia shook her head. "I don't think we'll be welcomed back."

"Well, we'd better go to the village," Rosetta said with a sigh. "At least we can tell the Low Ones what we've learned."

While they were talking, the sun had dipped below the horizon. The light was fading to darkness. They started to fly down toward the ground. But in the nighttime forest, they couldn't see more than a few inches in front of them.

Mia scraped against a branch. Rough bark scratched her skin. Nearby, she heard Lainey crashing among the branches, too.

"It's so dark. How are we ever going to find the Low Ones' village without any light?" Lainey asked.

In the darkness, Rosetta's glow was faintly visible beneath her cloak. Mia could see it flickering like a guttering candle. When fairies fell asleep, their glows went out. Mia could tell Rosetta was struggling to stay awake.

Mia felt exhausted, too. "How much farther do you think the ground is?" she asked.

"Close," said Lainey at the same time that Rosetta said, "Far."

There came the sound of twigs snapping. Mia heard Lainey say, "Ouch." There was a pause. Then she added, "Rosetta, can you come closer?"

Rosetta flew toward the sound of Lainey's voice. A second later, Mia saw a wall of twigs and sticks illuminated by her glow. Lainey had bumped into the giant nest.

"We could sleep here," Lainey suggested.

They studied the nest. Every bone in Mia's body longed to rest.

"What if the bird—or whatever built this—comes back?" Rosetta asked.

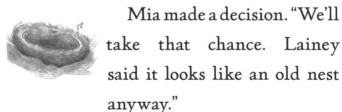 Mia made a decision. "We'll take that chance. Lainey said it looks like an old nest anyway."

They climbed in. The girls stretched

out. Rosetta found a comfortable spot on the edge of the nest. The twigs scratched her arms, but Mia hardly noticed.

The moment her head touched down, she fell right asleep.

Chapter 8

Ohhhhhhhhhhhh.

Rosetta's eyelids fluttered open. For a second she didn't know where she was. With a twinge of unease, she remembered. She was in a dark forest, on Shadow Island, far from Never Land. She could barely make out the faces of the girls sleeping nearby.

Rosetta sat up and looked around. Something had wakened her. What was it? She listened carefully.

High overhead, the treetops rustled, stirred by the wind. She heard the branches creaking and, beneath that, another sound.

Ohhhhhhhhhhhhhhhhh. A cross between a sigh and a groan came from somewhere above.

Rosetta flew out of the nest. Something somewhere needed her help.

Up, up she fluttered. The trees all around her seemed to be sleeping. But for some reason she wasn't afraid.

As she reached the treetops, the sound came again. Rosetta recognized Magnus, the tree they'd talked to earlier. His eyes were closed. His mouth opened wide in a moan.

"Great One," Rosetta said. "Is something wrong?"

The hollows of Magnus's eyes opened. He looked at Rosetta with fear. But a second later his face twisted in agony.

"An itch," he moaned. "A terrible itch!"

"Where?" Rosetta asked.

"By my middle limbs. *Ohhhhhh,*" the tree groaned. "Who can rest with such an awful itch?"

"Maybe I can help." Rosetta flew in a downward spiral, slowly circling the trunk.

Several feet down she heard a grinding sound. Rosetta located the source of the noise. A beetle was burrowing under the tree's bark.

"Go on! Get out of here, you little bully!" Rosetta kicked at the bark until the noise drove the beetle out. Then she flared her glow brightly to scare the beetle off.

When it was gone, Rosetta flew back up to Magnus.

"Oh, thank you." The tree sighed with relief. "That itch has been keeping me awake for days." His eyes focused on her.

"You spark, but you have no flame. What kind of fire are you?"

"My name is Rosetta," she told him. "And I'm not a fire. I'm a fairy."

"You are a friend to the Great Ones," Magnus said.

Rosetta nodded. "I'm a friend to all things that grow from the earth."

Magnus sighed again but said nothing more. Rosetta sat down on his nearest branch. They were silent together for a while. A low half-moon cast its light over the forest, turning the tops of the trees silver.

"It must be tiring, standing here for seven hundred years," Rosetta said after a time.

"It is," the tree said.

"But you must be very wise," Rosetta

added. "I'll bet you know everything about the forest."

Magnus was quiet for a moment. "I used to," he said at last. "When I was a sapling, I watched everything. I celebrated each egg in every nest. But the eggs hatched, and the hatchlings grew up and flew away. More came, and those left, too. After many years, I stopped paying attention. Everything comes and goes. The only things that remain the same are the sun, the moon, and the mountains. We Great Ones make the forest," he added, "but we know little of it."

"It sounds lonely," said Rosetta.

"I suppose," Magnus replied.

"Don't you talk to the other trees?"

"Sometimes," the tree replied. "But after hundreds of years, there's not much to say

anymore. Mostly I just rest and dream."

"What do you dream about?" Rosetta asked.

Magnus gazed beyond the treetops. "Flying," he said.

They sat in silence for a while longer. Rosetta wasn't sure if the tree was thinking or if he'd gone back to sleep. She rose and kissed him on his bark cheek. Then she started back down to her friends.

Rosetta flew slowly. The feeling of unease she'd had since they entered the forest was gone. Now she felt only a gentle sadness.

Poor tree, Rosetta thought. He was the greatest being in the forest. Yet he dreamed of what he couldn't have. What a long, lonely life. No wonder the trees seemed so gruff.

Chapter 9

Mia jolted awake. She'd dreamed she was falling again. She woke up just before she hit the ground.

She sat up, shivering. Gray light seeped through the trees. Lainey was still asleep next to her. Her mouth was open. A small white feather was stuck in one of her pigtails.

Mia gave her a shake to rouse her. Lainey sat up, fumbled for her glasses, and put them on. Then she took them off, polished them on her shirt, and put them on again. She blinked at Mia.

"What's going on?"

"It's morning. We'd better get back to the village," Mia said. "Everyone will be worried about us. Where's Rosetta?"

They looked all around the nest. "She's not here," Lainey said.

At once, terrible thoughts flooded Mia's mind. Had the trees somehow found Rosetta while they were sleeping? Or had some other creature snatched her? Maybe whatever had built the nest? But how had it gotten Rosetta without waking them?

Why had she ever thought it was a good idea to sleep here? And, why, oh why did they keep losing fairies?

"What should we do?" Lainey asked.

I don't know! Mia wanted to shout. *Can't you see I don't know?* Every decision she made seemed worse than the last. She wished Kate were there. Kate would know what to do.

As she scanned the forest, she saw a far-off pinprick of light. It was so faint that at first Mia thought she might be imagining it. But the light grew brighter and brighter. A tiny winged shape came into view.

"Rosetta!" the girls shouted with relief as the fairy landed on the edge of the nest.

"Quick, put on your hood! Before they see you," Mia urged. Rosetta's cloak had fallen back, and her glow shone radiantly.

But Rosetta hardly seemed to notice. Her face was lit up with excitement. "I've been talking with Magnus."

The girls gasped. "By *yourself*?" Lainey asked.

"They're not as terrible as they seem. They're just old and set in their ways. You might say their *bark* is worse than their bite." Rosetta laughed at her joke.

Then she told the girls about her

nighttime adventure. "I've been thinking," Rosetta said. "The Great Ones have a problem—beetles. If the Low Ones could keep the pests away, they could really help the trees."

"But why would they?" Lainey asked. "The Great Ones haven't done anything for them."

"That's the part I haven't figured out," Rosetta admitted. "We can tell the trees that not every light is a fire, but I don't think it will make a difference. They've kept themselves safe for hundreds of years by extinguishing every spark they see. I don't think they'd be willing to take any chances."

"So we haven't solved anything," Mia said with a sigh. "We'd better go give the sprites the bad news."

She stretched, feeling stiff from her night cramped in the nest. As she did, a slanted beam of sunlight came through the trees. It lay like a stripe across her arm. Mia stared at it. *If only more sunlight could reach the ground,* she thought, *the Low Ones would be so much better off.*

Mia dropped her arms. "That's it!" she exclaimed.

The others looked at her. "What?" Lainey asked.

It was so simple, Mia wondered why she hadn't thought of it before. "The trees can move to let the light through!"

"Trees *can't* move," Rosetta said.

"They can't move their *roots*," Mia said. "But they can move their branches. Remember how they swung them around when they got upset? And I'm almost sure a tree moved its branch to catch me when I fell."

"Why would it do that?" Lainey asked. "The Great Ones didn't seem to like us at all."

"Maybe they're nicer than we think," Mia said.

Rosetta nodded. "That's what I've been telling you. They're not unkind—they're just afraid, even though they don't seem it at first."

"So if the Low Ones keep the beetles away, the Great Ones will move their branches to give them more sunlight,"

Lainey said. "Do you think they'll both agree?"

"There's only one way to find out." Mia stood and looked at the treetops. It was such a long, long way up. *And a long way down,* Mia thought, remembering her fall.

She sat back down. "I can't go back up there."

"Why? What's wrong?" asked Lainey.

"I'm afraid," Mia admitted.

"Of the Great Ones?" Rosetta asked.

"Of flying." There. She'd said it. What would they think of her now?

"I know," Lainey told her.

Mia blinked. "You do?"

"Me too," Rosetta said.

"How?" Mia asked in astonishment. She thought she'd been so good at pretending.

"You get this super-scared look on your face right when we take off," Lainey told her.

"And when we're flying, you always ask 'How much farther?'" Rosetta added.

Mia burned with embarrassment. "Does Kate know, too? And Gabby? And the other fairies?"

Lainey shrugged. "Probably. It's not like we talk about it or anything. I always thought you were so brave."

"That's just it. I'm *not* brave," Mia said. "I'm a great big chicken."

Rosetta fluttered down and landed on her shoulder. "Everyone is scared of something—even the Great Ones. I don't think you're a chicken at all."

"No?" Mia asked.

"No," Rosetta said. "You're scared and yet you keep trying—that itself is courageous."

Mia thought about that. Was it possible she wasn't as cowardly as she thought?

She sighed and stood up. "Okay. Let's go make a deal."

✳

As soon as the Great Ones spotted the trio, an ominous rustling rippled through their boughs.

"Spark," they murmured. "The spark is back!"

Uh-oh, Mia thought. "Get ready to bolt," she whispered to her friends.

But then the giant tree Magnus spoke up. "Quiet your limbs," he told the other trees. "She is a flameless spark."

"A spark with no flame?" a nearby tree rumbled. "How can that be?"

Rosetta removed the cloak so her glow could be fully seen. "Because I'm a fairy," she said. "A garden-talent fairy. We want to help you."

"Let us hear what she has to say," Magnus said.

A few trees grumbled, but their branches stopped shaking.

"We know you have a problem with beetles," Rosetta said.

At the mention of beetles, a few of the trees groaned.

"We told you about the Low Ones who live below," Mia spoke up. "We think they can help you. They will guard you against beetles. In return you must give them light."

"How?" asked Magnus.

"Easy," said Lainey. "If you part your branches a little, the sunlight can reach the ground."

The trees were silent for a long time. *Are they speaking to one another through their roots?* Mia wondered.

Finally, Magnus sighed. "All right," he said. "We agree."

Lainey gave Mia's hand a squeeze. They'd done it! "Come on," she said. "Let's go tell the Low Ones."

"Wait," Mia said. Her heart was beating fast. Did she dare push her luck with the Great Ones? She turned back to Magnus. "First, show us that you can do it."

There was another long silence. She heard wood creaking. Then, ever so slowly, the trees' branches began to rise.

Inch by inch, little by little, the branches parted. As they did, shafts of sunlight fell through to the forest floor.

They stayed like that for a long time.

"Okay," Mia said with a nod. "That will do."

Chapter 10

Back in the sprites' village, they found Kate, Gabby, and Iridessa waiting in the old tree stump with Ersa and several sprites. Kate looked much better than she had the day before. When she saw them, she jumped up, exclaiming, "Where have you been?"

"We were up all night worrying!" Iridessa added.

Mia, Lainey, and Rosetta told them

what had happened. When they got to the part where the trees spoke, Kate couldn't keep quiet.

"Talking trees!" she interrupted. "I can't believe I missed that."

Gabby squeezed Mia's hand. "Was it scary?"

"At first," Mia said. "But the trees turned out to be not so scary after all."

They told Ersa and the sprites about the deal they'd come up with. "Do you think the Low Ones could keep the beetles away?" Rosetta asked.

Ersa lifted her chin proudly, taking in the shafts of sunlight that had already begun to shine through. "The Low Ones are great warriors. Tell the Great Ones we will accept their offer."

"No," Mia said.

Everyone looked at her. "No?" said Ersa.

"Tell them yourself," Mia said.

The sprite looked flustered. "Us? Talk to the Great Ones?"

Mia smiled. "I'm the world's biggest scaredy-cat. If I can do it, so can you."

*

"Are you sure this is safe?" Ersa asked. The sprite was sitting in Mia's cupped palm. Clinging tightly to her thumb, she peered over the edge of Mia's hand.

"Trust me," Mia told her. "I do it all the time. But one piece of advice," she added as the ground receded behind them. "Don't look down."

As they flew toward the tree canopy,

Mia glanced over at Kate. Two sprites
were riding on each of Kate's shoulders.
Mia laughed. "Not to worry you," she told
her, "but you have Low Ones coming out
of your ears."

Kate grinned back. Her eyes were bright
and her face had regained its normal color.
The only sign that she'd been injured was
a small purple bruise on her forehead.

Lainey and Gabby were both carrying sprites, too. The girls had decided that since the Great Ones would never be able to come down to the ground, the only way they would ever meet was to bring the sprites to them.

The fairies had come along, too. Rosetta led the way. Mia had the feeling she was looking forward to talking with the Great Ones again.

When they reached the treetops, Mia wondered if they'd made a mistake. The trees regarded them with their usual scowls. But a second later, they broke into gentle smiles.

"So, it's you again," Magnus said.

"We brought some friends to meet

you," Rosetta told him. She gave them a nod.

Mia flew forward. She held Ersa up so Magnus could see her. "This is Ersa and her friends." She gestured to the other sprites. "They are the ones who will help you."

Magnus and Ersa gazed at each other with curiosity. "Hello, Little One," the tree said in his slow, deep voice.

Ersa bowed. "Greetings, Great One. We thank you for giving light back to us."

Magnus looked abashed. "I didn't realize I had ever taken it."

Nearby, other sprites were talking to other trees. Mia heard them talking about the forest and the different ways they saw it, from above and below. When it was time for the sprites to return home, they said good-bye with real fondness.

"He was a good Great One," Ersa said as they flew back down.

"I think so, too," Mia said.

When they landed in the sprites' village, it was still bathed in sunlight.

"Soon there will be flowers," Ersa said. "Our village will be bright, like yours."

"We're glad to help," Rosetta replied.

"But now you must tell us about our friend Tinker Bell," Mia reminded her.

Ersa nodded. "I told you the truth when I said I hadn't seen her."

Mia's heart sank. Had they gone to all that trouble for nothing?

"But," the sprite went on, "not two days ago some of our scouts saw a light moving through the forest. It was gone before they could reach it. But it looked like one of you."

Gabby clapped her hands. "That must have been Tink!"

"Which way was she going?" Iridessa asked.

"East." Ersa pointed. But among the tall trees, every direction looked the same.

"Can you show us?" Kate asked.

Ersa spoke to some of the sprites. Three with spotted caps and asparagus spears stepped forward. "They will take you as far as the edge of the woods," Ersa told the girls and fairies.

They said good-bye to Ersa, who wished them well on their journey.

As they followed the trio of sprites,

Mia noticed that although the forest surrounding the village was still dark, it didn't seem nearly as scary as it had the day before.

Soon the trees began to grow farther apart. When they came to a point where they could see open sky, the sprites stopped. The girls and fairies stopped, too. They'd reached the end of the forest.

"What's out there?" Iridessa wondered. She turned to ask the sprites. But they were already gone.

"So much for saying good-bye," Kate said.

"Oh, look!" Gabby cried suddenly.

A bright spot of light hovered among the trees. It hung there uncertainly, as if it was trying to decide whether to enter the forest.

Mia's breath caught. It was the size and shape of a fairy. Could it be . . . ?

A second light joined it. The two lights came closer.

"Fawn! Silvermist!" everyone exclaimed.

"I can't believe we finally found you!" Silvermist cried. "We've been looking everywhere."

"How did you get here?" Rosetta asked in astonishment. "We lost you in the storm!"

"When you disappeared, we followed you," Fawn told them. "But that's not important right now. Listen, we saw something—"

Silvermist buzzed in excited circles, exclaiming, "We think we know where to find Tink!"